Anonymous

The Life and Labors of Eliza R. Snow Smith

With a full account of her funeral services

Anonymous

The Life and Labors of Eliza R. Snow Smith
With a full account of her funeral services

ISBN/EAN: 9783337256876

Printed in Europe, USA, Canada, Australia, Japan

Cover: Foto ©Raphael Reischuk / pixelio.de

More available books at **www.hansebooks.com**

THE

LIFE AND LABORS

— OF —

ELIZA R. SNOW SMITH;

WITH   FULL ACCOUNT OF HER

FUNERAL SERVICES.

———

PUBLISHED AT
THE JUVENILE INSTRUCTOR OFFICE,
SALT LAKE CITY, UTAH.
1888.

PREFACE.

THERE is no apology necessary for the publication of this little pamphlet containing a brief account of the labors of so eminent a lady as Sister Eliza R. Snow Smith. Her diligent and unceasing exertions to promote the cause of truth in the earth have endeared her to every Latter-day Saint, and especially to the sisters among whom she was constantly working. For the purpose of preserving in a compact form an account of the life and labors of this noble woman, this publication is issued, and not with the view of making money, as the price at which it is sold is barely sufficient to pay its cost.

THE PUBLISHERS.

ELIZA R. SNOW SMITH.

MONDAY morning, December 5th, at five minutes past one o'clock, in her apartments in the Lion House, this city, there passed away to the Paradise of God, the spirit of one of the noblest, best and purest women that ever graced the earth —Eliza R. Snow Smith.

The news of this event will cause no surprise in the community, as it was generally known that the deceased had been gradually failing for the last year. She was not affected with any special disease, the complaint being simply a decline of the physical powers, superinduced by old age.

Sister Smith's case was a remarkable instance of the power of mind over matter, her mental clearness never forsaking her a moment; she was conscious up to within five minutes of the end. About ten o'clock, Patriarch John Smith, who frequently called during her sickness, was by her bedside, and inquired if she recognized him. The customary smile lit up the beautiful countenance, and the reply came in clear and distinct tones—

"Of course I do." He blessed her, and she ex‐pressed her thankfulness.

Her brother, Apostle Lorenzo Snow, has been with her a great deal, and was by her side when she breathed her last. Between the brother and sister there has ever existed a most exquisite affection, that has never been interrupted by any incident during the long course of their lives.

Aunt Eliza, as she was familiarly called, has felt for some time the probability of her passing to the sphere beyond, and that same resignation which characterized her course in all the dispensations of providence was conspicuous in relation to her approaching dissolution. In the presence of the writer a few days ago, she said, in substance: "I have no choice as to whether I shall die or live. I am perfectly willing to go or stay, as our Heavenly Father shall order. I am in His hands." While she spoke, her wonderfully lustrous, dark eyes shone with more than earthly brightness, and as she conversed with those around her, the native intelligence which has so strongly individualized her, was remarkably exhibited, considering the weakness of her body.

The deceased was slightly above medium height and of slender build; her bearing was at once graceful and dignified. Hers was a noble countenance, the forehead being unusually high and expansive, and the features, of a slightly Hebrew cast, exquisitely cut as those of an artistic specimen of the sculptor's art. The most striking feature of all were those wonderful eyes, deep, penetrating, full of meaning and intelligence, often illumined with poetic fire. They were indeed the windows of a noble soul.] Her conversation was charming, every word being distinctly articulated, while her sentences were admirably constructed. In speech and action she was thoughtful and deliberate. While of susceptible and delicate organism, and in every way womanly, she had great decision of character. So deep were her convictions and potent her sense of morality, that we believe she would more readily have surrendered her life than acted in opposition to them.

Deceased was the daughter of Oliver and Rosetta Leonora Pettibone Snow, and was born January 21st, 1804, in Becket, Berkshire County, Massachusetts. She was consequently aged eighty-three years, ten months and fourteen days. She was the second in a family of seven children, and was of unmixed Puritan stock, all lines of her ancestry running back through pure streams of New England blood. The Snow family from which she was descended was of Massachusetts, while her mother's family, the Pettibones, was of Connecticut. During her infancy, her parents removed to Mantua, Portage County, Ohio, where five more children were born to them. Her father was a farmer by occupation, but much of his time was devoted to public business, and he was under the necessity of enlisting her services in the capacity of secretary, a species of employment for which her natural capabilities rendered her well adapted.

She was well skilled in household accomplishments, such as needlework and the like, but she possessed a literary talent which was destined to eclipse all commonplace acquirements. In early youth she began writing poems for various publications, and had won quite a reputation among some of the publishers whom she had favored with the productions of her pen. This is sufficiently attested by the circumstance of her being requested to write, for publication, a requiem for John Adams and Thomas Jefferson, whose simultaneous death on the nation's natal day, 1826, afforded to the young authoress a theme well fitted for the lofty and patriotic spirit that always characterized her muse. The appearance of this poem, written when she was but twenty-two years of age, was an event that ushered her into fame.

She was thoroughly and carefully educated in the best schools of the region in which she was reared, and in her girlhood became acquainted with Alexander Campbell, the noted scholar and theologian, and founder of the Campbellite sect; and also with Walter Scott and Sidney Rigdon, able co-laborers with Mr. Campbell. These were men of erudition, and they took pains to assist her in the study of the Scriptures, especially the prophecies of the Old Testament. It is probable that her scriptural studies under their tuition, aided in preparing her mind to receive the gospel in its fullness.

Early in the year 1835, Sister Eliza's elder sister visited the Saints at Kirtland, and was deeply impressed with their teachings. Her testimony caused Sister Eliza to fear that the news of the proclamation of the gospel by the Prophet Joseph was too joyful to be true. She pursued her investigations for a short time with increasing faith, and at length was baptized April 5th, 1835. In the following December she removed to Kirtland and became an inmate of the Prophet Joseph's household, boarding with his family and teaching a select school for young ladies.

On New Year's Day, 1837, a painful scene took place in which she was the central figure, and which is virtually described in her poem "What it is to be a Saint." On that day she bade farewell to her home, the fond associations of youth and the flattering prospects that were opening before her, being fully determined to unite forever her fortunes with those of the persecuted Saints. It is supposed that she wrote the poem referred to about this time, and that in it are shown forth mental struggles and experiences of her own. She returned to the home of the Prophet, became governess to his children, and was companion to his wife Emma for a number of years.

Her intimate association with Joseph the Seer, ripened into a holy consummation, and she, in the year 1843, became his wife in accordance with the sacred ordinance of heaven, and the direct command of God to her husband. She thus became one of the first women of this dispensation to enter the sacred and divine order of plural marriage.

She generously gave her patrimony for the

completion of the Kirtland Temple, and when the
Saints there, yielding to the pressure of the persecution which raged with increased fierceness after
the dedication of that structure, removed west-
ward, she accompanied them, locating first at Far
West and afterward at Adam-ondi-Ahman, in
Missouri. To recount that portion of her life
which was passed in Missouri, would be but to
repeat the oft told tale of persecution, wrong and
outrage to which the Saints there were subjected.
Suffice it to say that Sister Eliza bore a part in
some of the most prominent and painful scenes
that go to make up the history of those times,
and shared in the exodus of the Saints to Illinois.
She stopped for a short time at Quincy, and after-
wards went to Lima, supporting herself by needlework.

In the summer of 1839, Sidney Rigdon sent for
her to go to Nauvoo to teach his family school,
and that city was her home until the expulsion
from it of the people of her choice. During those
years a lofty and prophetic as well poetical inspiration seemed almost constantly to rest upon her,
and shines forth in radiant power in the poems
written by her during that period.

In the first organization of a Relief Society,
effected in Nauvoo under the personal supervision
of the Prophet Joseph Smith, Sister Eliza was
chosen secretary and in the organization of those
same beneficent institutions in the various stakes
and wards of the Church, since it located in the
mountains, her's has been in her womanly sphere,

the leading part. In connection with her labors among the Relief Societies, she was long and actively engaged in organizing the Young Ladies' Mutual Improvement and Primary Associations, taking almost, if not quite as prominent, a part in the work of their establishment, as in that of the Relief Societies.

Early in February, 1846, Sister Smith crossed the Mississippi River, on the occasion of the third great exodus from their homes of her people since her connection with them. She was traveling with the family of Colonel Stephen Markham, a staunch friend of her husband's, and certain incidents and misfortunes occurred to the party which rendered it necessary for Sister Smith to drive an ox team from Mt. Pisgah to the Missouri River. At Winter Quarters she suffered terribly from exposure and sickness, and at one time lay nigh unto death. Early in June, 1847, she started from Winter Quarters, with the family of Brother Robert Pierce, and in the company led by Jedediah M. Grant, on the weary journey to Great Salt Lake Valley, following closely in the wake of the pioneers. She arrived at her journey's end early in October. President Brigham Young provided her a home with his family immediately after her arrival, and she thereafter continued an inmate of his household.

Among the prominent events in the life of Sister Smith was her journey to and from Palestine, made in company with President George A. Smith, Apostle Lorenzo Snow, and other prominent brethren.   The party left Salt Lake City. in the fall of 1872, and returned in June, 1873.   The trip is described in a volume of nearly four hundred pages, entitled "Correspondence of Palestine Tourists," being a compilation of letters written by members of the party.   To this work the deceased contributed largely, her correspondence manifesting keen observation and graphic discriptive powers.

The inspiration which vitalized her pen, and brought from it words as imperishable as the language, was not suppressed even under the most trying and adverse circumstances; and at frequent intervals of her weary journey she produced poems of rare beauty.

Our sister is not dead; she simply sleeps, her intelligent part having gone to that bright sphere where the just await the time of their redemption, when there will be a reunion of the spirit with the body through the power of the resurrection. Having slept in peace, she has secured her title to be among the heavenly throng that will accompany the Lord of glory when He shall come to this creation to take the reins of its government. She has gone to mingle with the righteous who have kept the faith; to associate with her husband, the great Prophet of the last dispensation, to whom she has shown a sublime devotion that will be appreciated in the eternities to come.   She was beloved here, where the memory of her virtues will be cherished, so is she beloved in the sphere to which she has passed.

In a sense she is with us yet. The work she accomplished remains, and its fruits will multiply, as truth begets truth in an unceasing round. The part which she took under the direction of the Priesthood in organizing the little children, the young ladies and the members of her sex of all ages, and forwarding the work of instruction among them still exists, and her spirit permeates all these beneficent associations. Her charitable deeds in administering to the sick, the afflicted and bowed down, still live and bear their fruits, and there are other noble spirits who will continue to carry forward the multiplication of good of the same nature. They have been her faithful associates and counselors while she was in life, and they will continue to emulate the virtues and noble traits with which her whole career has been fruitful to an extraordinary degree.

There was a marked harmony between the qualities of the heart and the gifts of the intellect of this remarkable woman. She was a poet of the first order, all her poetic productions being of a most exalted character. Some of them are as sublime as ever were penned. One alone, which has been sung times without number, would be sufficient to establish her fame in this direction. The opening lines are:

> O my Father, thou that dwellest
> In the high and glorious place !
> When shall I regain thy presence,
> And again behold thy face?

In thy holy habitation,
   Did my spirit once reside?
In my first primeval childhood,
   Was I nurtured near thy side?

The foregoing poetical embodiment of the doctrine of pre-existence of spirits is not more striking than the thoughts enclosed in the concluding lines:

In the heavens are parents single?
   No; the thought makes reason stare!
Truth is reason; truth eternal
   Tells me I've a mother there.

The purity of her life and nature necessarily rendered her a fit medium through whom the Holy Ghost could manifest those gifts and graces of the gospel of the Redeemer that characterized the disciple of the Church of Christ in ancient times and which also exist in it as revealed anew in this dispensation. It was delightful to the Saints to listen to the exercise by her of the gift of tongues, accompanied always by an influence of inexpressible sweetness and comfort, or to hear her give the interpretation of the manifestations of the same gift operating through herself and others. She also exhibited on occasions the prophetic power. The latest of her predictions in this regard was to the effect that a time of severe trial for the Saints was approaching, beyond which there was a glorious outcome for the faithful. It may be said concerning her that she was indeed "an elect lady."—*Deseret News.*

FUNERAL SERVICES.

THE funeral rites over the remains of Sister E. R. Snow Smith were conducted on Friday, Dec. 7th, Pres. Angus M. Cannon presiding. Between eleven and twelve o'clock the pall-bearers assembled at the Lion House and conveyed the body, which was enclosed in a neat casket of polished natural wood, to the Assembly Hall, followed by relatives and immediate friends. The congregation assembled there was very large, the building being filled.

The various stands were, in accordance with the wish of the departed, draped in white, nothing black being introduced. There was a great variety of floral offerings, contributed by loving hearts. They were of various forms, such as wreaths, crosses, hearts and other suggestive and appropriate devices. At noon President Cannon called the congregation to order. The choir sang:

I know that my Redeemer lives;

The opening prayer was offered by Bishop Alexander McRae.

The choir sang that beautiful production of the deceased:

"O my Father, thou that dwellest
In the high and glorious place!
When shall I regain thy presence,
And again behold thy face?
In thy holy habitation,
Did my spirit once reside?

In my first primeval childhood,
  Was I nurtured near thy side?

"For a wise and glorious purpose
  Thou hast placed me here on earth,
And withheld the recollection
  Of my former friends and birth;
Yet oft-times a secret something
  Whispered, You're a stranger here;
And I felt that I had wandered
  From a more exalted sphere.

"I had learned to call thee Father,
  Through thy spirit from on high;
But, until the Key of Knowledge
  Was restored, I knew not why.
In the heavens are parents single?
  No; the thought makes reason stare!
Truth is reason; truth eternal
  Tells me, I've a mother there.

"When I leave this frail existence,
  When I lay this mortal by,
Father, mother, may I meet you
  In your royal court on high?
Then, at length, when I've completed
  All you sent me forth to do,
With your mutual approbation
  Let me come and dwell with you."

PRESIDENT ANGUS M. CANNON

then said: The hymn just sang in our hearing contains expressions of adoration and devotion to our God. Sister Eliza R. Snow Smith who lies before us, or whose earthly remains are now contained in the casket before us, was one who was well fitted and qualified to come upon the earth at the period of time she did—a time when certain noble spirits whom God had permitted to come forth from His presence to usher in, upon a world that lay in darkness, the gospel of Jesus Christ, were here upon the earth. ᵗFrom the time she first heard the inspired utterances fall from the lips of the Prophet Joseph her heart responded to the call, feeling it an honor to help sustain those whom God had raised up to enlighten mankind and proclaim redemption to a fallen world. ˙In adversity as in prosperity her soul adored her Maker.ˣ Her poetic muse took the most lofty flights, often while sitting with others around the camp-fire, often while su'fering the deepest distress and greatest sorrow. Her heart continually rejoiced in knowing that her Redeemer lived, and that men had been raised up to preach and expound the plan of salvation to the human family, and to establish God's kingdom in power upon the earth. When her voice has been heard, it has been heard stimu-.lating her sisters to glorify their Creator, and to feel thankful that they had been permitted to take part in so great a work. It has been the good fortune and happiness of your servant, who now addresses you, to be intimately acquainted during the past year, more so than it has been his privilege in former years, with the deceased; although when a little boy—associated with the people of Nauvoo and of this city—he was accustomed to look upon her as one of the fairest, one of the purest, highest-minded, noble women that God had created. He was happy in knowing that she was counted worthy to be the wife of the great Prophet and Seer, God's servant Joseph Smith. She was ever calm and peaceful and submissive to his divine counsels, submitting her will to his will as he submitted his will to the will of God our Heavenly Father.   He suffered his innocent blood to be shed to seal the testimony he had given us and make it in force for the redemption of mankind. She made her life to conform with that of her partner.   She loved to serve him.   She loved also to teach her sisters the principle of self-sacrifice, which they had exhibited in the midst of trials and sufferings and joy.   Her heart pulsated with the fond hope that she might live many years to stimulate her sisters in the works of righteousness, and to plead with them to avoid the evils and vanities of Babylon.   She desired that they should submit their will to the calling of wives, mothers, sisters and daughters of the Israel of God. She often spoke of the trials that awaited us, and said that trials must necessarily come upon us from the nature of the calling that God has called us to. When she found her bodily strength giving way, and felt she must succumb to the monster death, her heart glorified God that she would be numbered with the people of God, and I assured her that she would ever remain dear in the memory of the people of God, and that they would rejoice in knowing that they will yet enjoy her society in the endless future. At this assurance a smile came over her face which I cannot forget.   All her desire was that her sisters would be able to resist temptation, and live worthy of the fellowship of God.   Peace be to her ashes. Her soul will rest in peace. Her fondest expectations will be realized. May her sisters emulate her example for ever and ever is my prayer in the name of Jesus, Amen.

ELDER JOSEPH C. KINGSBURY.

Brethren and Sisters: I can endorse every word that Brother Cannon has spoken here this morning. This sister has now left us. She has gone to rest. She has made her calling and election sure. She was one of the earliest to embrace the new and everlasting covenant. She has made a sacrifice that God accepts. So must we also be ready and willing to do the same when we are called upon to do so. We are called to pass through persecution, trials and tribulation, but what are these things compared to the glories to be attained hereafter. Let us seek diligently to make our calling and elections sure. We have to work, to be diligent in all things, both spiritual and temporal. We must endeavor to overcome every evil and every temptation. The enemy is on the alert. He desires to destroy the Saints of God. But let us be united, and the powers of darkness cannot have influence over us. Our trust is in God, and He will deliver us. This is my prayer in the name of Jesus, Amen.

ELDER J. B. NOBLE.

I feel grateful for the opportunity of bearing testimony to the very truthful remarks that have been spoken in relation to our sister who lies before us, or her remains. I can endorse every sentiment, and further, I can bear record that from

an early day, from the commencement of her connection with this work, I have been familiar with
her labors; and I was favored above measure in her
society across the desert, from Nauvoo to this place.
I enjoyed her confidence, and my heart is filled
with joy unspeakable in having the opportunity to
bear my testimony to her life which has been one
of the very highest grade, prepared, as has been
said by President Cannon, to come forth in this
dispensation, and to do a mighty work. She has
accomplished that work in the fullest sense, and
the time draws near, the hour is nigh, when she
will hear the voice of her sleeping companion,
him who laid down his life for the cause of God,
and shed his blood for the same. She will soon
hear his voice, for the period has rolled around.
It behooves us who have named the name of the
Lord, taken upon us the name of Saints, to look
into our hearts and see if we possess the principle
pertaining to the higher law—namely, to do unto
others as we would have others do unto us.   We
should bless the human family that are ignorant
in relation to this great and glorious work with
which we are associated. In relation to the deceased, we should feel to ask the blessing of the
Lord upon her relatives, and upon her sisters who
are honest in heart, that they may, with firm will,
practice those principles that she has.   And
may the honest among all people be awakened to
a realizing sense that this latter-day work is none
other than the work Jehovah predicted from all
time that should precede the coming of the Son

of Man. Let us be wise; do the bidding of the
Holy Priesthood; work out our salvation by living
the law of the gospel, and eternal riches, eternal
exaltation, and eternal glory will be our portion,
our happy lot. I ask this in the name of Jesus,
Amen.

ELDER JACOB GATES.

I am glad to have the opportunity of bearing my
testimony to what has already been said. It is
truly a joy and satisfaction to the living to see
such a congregation assembled as we see now before us to pay—shall I say the last respects to our
departed sister? It seems to me an improper term,
from the fact that we shall long remember our sister and her virtues, and I hope we shall endeavor
to practice the same while we are permitted to
live upon the earth. I have known sister Eliza
R. Snow Smith for many years. I have been
somewhat familiar with her personally, as she paid
many visits to my house, in the course of which we
had many pleasant conversations. The deceased,
among the representative women of this last dispensation, seemed to be second to none. Morally, relig-
iously and poetically, she seemed to be one of those
perfect women that was prepared for the age, and to
represent her sex in this great latter-day work,
and she nobly filled the mission for which she was
appointed, and in which she took her place in the
early days of this Church. I pray our Heavenly
Father that we may all emulate her virtues and
cultivate the faith that she so nobly maintained

through all the difficulties and trials of life
through which she and this people have passed,
never faltering. /In all the conversations I ever
had with her, her faith reached onward and up-
ward to the very climax of human perfection of
ideas in regard to the great work in which she was
engaged/ I hope and pray that we may be equally
humble and faithful, and honor the memory of
our dear departed ones. Our brethren and sisters
are passing away constantly, and we may expect
in the near future that there will be but a very
few on the earth who were familiar or were acquainted with the Prophet, Joseph Smith. May
that spirit that bears record of the Father and
Son bear record of the truth of this great latter-
day work, and we shall soon see consummated the
purposes of God as He has ordained. What we are
now passing through is what we as Latter-day
Saints have long been looking for. It has been
predicted by prophets and apostles and by those
who were inspired by the spirit of revelation in
years gone by, to my certain knowledge, and we
need not look upon our present condition as anything new or strange in the progress and develop-
ment of this great latter-day work. Trials must
necessarily come to purify and prove the Saints in
their faith and confidence in the Lord, and our
enemies will be given an opportunity to fill up
their cup of iniquity and to prepare themselves
for the judgments that God has decreed must come
sooner or later, upon those who fight Zion and
seek to destroy her. May we be humble and gird

on the whole armor of God, and eventually be
saved in the kingdom of God, which I pray may
be the case with us all, in the name of Jesus,
Amen. ´

APOSTLE JOHN W. TAYLOR.

I am thankful to hear the eulogies of my breth-
. ren who have had many years' experience with
the deceased.   I have known Sister Smith by
reputation from my infancy, though I had not
any personal acquaintance save by way of introduc-
tion. I feel concerning our sister that she has finished
her work, and that she will gain salvation in the.
kingdom of God.   All others who are worthy will
gain the same blessing.   None can gain more
than this: The Savior says: "Let your light so
shine before men, that they may see your good
works, and glorify your Father which is in heav-
en."   I feel that the works of Sister Smith are before us all.   We can pattern after them with pro-
fit.   He that hath eternal life is rich.   The Savior said, "Such riches are free to all those who
keep the commandments of God."   When the
Savior commanded His apostles to "Go into all
the world and preach the gospel to every crea-
ture.   He that believeth and is baptized shall be
saved; he that believeth not shall be damned,"
He meant what he said.   Our sister has embraced
the everlasting gospel, and she is entitled to the
blessing that the Savior and Redeemer of the
world promised.   The Savior also said, "And
every one that hath forsaken houses, or brethren,

or sisters, or father, or mother, or wife, or children, or lands, for my name's sake, shall receive an
hundred fold, and shall inherit everlasting life."
We have the word "mother" mentioned here. It is
known among us that George Washington is called
the "Father of his country" though he died without
children.   Yet through the devotion of the Ameri-
can people he has earned the name of Father.
Inasmuch as the deceased was deprived of bearing children, she is entitled to be called Mother
among this people, just as much as George Washington is to be called Father by the people of the
United States. ⸗She has been a mother to this
people⸗ She has passed through trials and tribulations. ·She has made us joyful by her poetical
effusions; we have sorrowed when she sorrowed,
and we have rejoiced when she rejoiced.   I pray
that all who have seen her good works may endeavor to emulate them, and thus receive the reward of the just.   I do not desire to lengthen my
remarks. ⸗I pray God the Eternal Father that
whenever we think of Eliza R. Snow Smith, we
will not think of her as "Aunt Eliza" in the future,
but that we may in truth and righteousness call her
Mother.⸗

ELDER MILO ANDRUS.

It is with gratitude and great thanksgiving in my
heart that I am permitted to say a few words on
this present occasion, having had the acquaintance of Sister Eliza for the last forty-five years, or
thereabouts; and having never a speck, or a blot,

or anything that would indicate a misstep in all her life, and having been comforted and cheered by her good counsels and advice, I feel to bear my testimony to the virtue and goodness and integrity of her heart while upon this earth. This might be considered by some a day of mourning. I do not so consider it. I know the reluctance of relatives to part with friends, and perhaps they may look upon this occasion as a time of mourning. But I cannot feel that way. My whole being magnifies the name of my God when I reflect upon the wise counsels and instructions of the departed. In relation to what the brethren have said in regard to her being Mother, I bear my testimony that thousand and tens of thousands will call her Mother in Israel and enjoy her society forever and ever. We have a subject before us that has fulfilled the royal law of God as far as it has been revealed. Indeed, when she meets her entire acts upon this earth, she is one of that class that can face her record and look at it complacently. She has acted an honorable part, and her deeds will secure unto her the highest exaltation in the eternal worlds. Under these circumstances there cannot be any death, cannot be any mourning, but our sympathies on the present occasion are drawn out exceedingly, especially the sympathies of those who have been benefited by her wise instructions, and made to rejoice in the beautiful songs that God inspired her to give unto Israel. If we had had one before us that had denied the faith, we might bow our heads in mourning; but

on the present occasion we have one who has
gained eternal salvation, and it is to be hoped that
the Israel of God will endeavor to emulate her
example and fulfill the measure of their being
upon this earth. Many thousands of the sisters in
Israel who prized her instructions will feel
sad on this occasion, but they know that the
deceased has merely gone to sleep; it is a death
here and birth there. Every heart is raised with
thanksgiving when we contemplate her life among
the Saints of the Most High. In the deepest
of her tribulations, I never heard such a thing
as a murmur fall from the lips of the deceased.
Such a statement could be made of very few. I
am afraid there is a large per cent of the Latter-
day Saints who could say that their feelings gave
way once in a while. But let us follow the
example of our sister, and carry out the whole law
of God, that we may have joy with her in our
future state. I feel pleased in the contemplation
as to where our sister has gone—not pleased that
she has gone from our presence, but pleased to think
of the society she has gone to embrace, the God-
like men and women who have gone before us,
and I expect ere long to join that heavenly choir
and enjoy the society of those I love. May God
add His blessings upon the relatives and acquaint-
ances of the deceased. May we endeavor to emulate her example, and do the will of God on earth
as it is done in the heaven, which I ask in the
name of Jesus, Amen.

Words of eulogy will fail to add anything to the well-known characteristics of Sister Eliza Snow, who has departed this life. She has been known in this Church, I suppose, from the beginning. She is known to the present generation. She has been known in her official capacity from the city of Nauvoo to these mountains, and she is known to the offspring of the fathers in Israel in this present generation. What I might say of my acquaintance with her, I presume, would not add a straw to the good feeling towards and confidence in Sister Eliza. She has inherited the riches of eternal life, which are the greatest gift of God. She has added her testimony in a great many ways to this work—in literary works, by her own voice, and more especially has she borne testimony to the work of the last days in her examples. Precept is a very good thing; we can talk a great deal; but examples tell, and Sister Eliza's example has had far more power and influence than her precept has had, although, so far as I know in my associations with her in my family, her precepts have ever been worthy of emulation. This audience are acquainted with these facts, and it is but very little use to repeat them further than to bear our testimony to the goodness of Sister Eliza. Peace be to Sister Eliza, and to her dust, and to her name; and let us endeavor to so live that we may enjoy her society behind the vail — meet her with Joseph and Hyrum, and with David Patten and with other martyrs that have passed behind the vail, for the gospel's sake.   That we may be able to follow her example, and secure the same glory, which is eternal, is my prayer in the name of Jesus, Amen.

ELDER JOHN NICHOLSON.

Brother Smoot and the other brethren who have spoken on this interesting occasion have expressed my thoughts and views in reference to our beloved sister as well, if not better, than I have the power to express them myself.   It is our duty, in common with that of all others, to devote ourselves thoroughly and completely to the work of bringing our condition into harmony with the truth of our Heavenly Father.   In order to do this it is needful that we cultivate that power we have inherited from Him, to grasp and comprehend the truth, and when it is in us and our thoughts are occupied in the contemplation of it, we have within us the thought that is in the mind of God.   He is the fountain of life and intelligence.   It is especially necessary that we should bring our moral natures into unison with the truth when we comprehend it, and also that our sympathies should extend to all the creatures that have been formed by the God of heaven.   In none of these respects, according to my opinion and my conviction, which is deep rooted, was our sister deficient. She had a mind of uncommon brightness and capacity; she was continually endeavoring to make it the storehouse of the truths of time and eternity, and she also exercised the great gifts which she possessed, not for her own benefit, but for the benefit of others, not hiding her light under a bushel, but shedding its rays upon all those who came within her sphere or in contact with her. Those truths that dwelt in her mind were embodied, as has been already stated, in a literary form, and .they are now left to us, many of them, as a legacy, clothed in all the beauty that chaste language and exquisite imagery give them] Her morality was, according to all that was known of her, spotless, and it was exhibited, as has been stated already, by a constant effort to impress upon her sisters and all her associates the necessity of their conduct being in strict line with the principles of righteousness. [Her works exhibit the comforting fact that she had a heart that could feel for . another. Sympathy was one of her leading characteristics; consequently she exhibited· in her career that true religion, the essence of religion, that is admirable wherever it is seen. She was found by the side of the sick, administering comfort to those who were afflicted, and consoling those who were bowed down in grief.] In fact I will say that as she was a poet of great excellence, the greatest production in this respect that she has given to the world has been her life, which has been a poem from its commencement to its close. May peace be with her ashes, and comfort rest upon those who remain is the prayer of a sincere friend who loved Sister Eliza.

BIHOP O. F. WHITNEY.

I shall not attempt to say the hundredth part of
what I feel on this occasions, for I have neither the
time nor the inclination to do so.   It fell to my lot
in connection with a number of the brethren, on
two occasions during the last illness of Sister Eliza,
to place my hands upon her head, at her request,-
and bless her in the name of the Lord; and I could
not help but mark the free flow of the Spirit and
the great desire which welled up in our hearts to
bless her with all things spiritual and temporal.
It seemed as though there was no end to the
promises which we felt to make her, and it is my
testimony that she was worthy of all that any man
of God or woman of God ever felt to place upon
her head; and the proof is, not only in her life,
which is before us, and before the world, and the
love and confidence of her associates, but in this
sanction and approval of the Spirit of God, which
never yet sanctioned that which was false or
deceptive.   I regard our departed sister as one of
the noble and great ones of God, one of those
spoken of by Father Abraham, who said, "The
Lord had shown unto me, Abraham, the intelli-
gences that were organized before the world was;
and among all these there were many of the noble
and great ones; and God saw these souls that they
were good, and he stood in the midst of them and
he said, These will I make my rulers."   It fell to
the lot of Sister Eliza to be honored of God and
of man.   It is not always given to these noble
spirits to be so distinguished or so much thought

of in the world. Some walk the streets in rags; some may sit upon thrones; some are among the lowly and some among the high; some are rich and others poor; but whether men honor them or not, they are the honored and chosen of God nevertheless; they are His jewels, which He will gather up when He comes. It was Sister Eliza's fortune, not only to hold position, not only to be honored with public trust, but to wisely use that trust, that power and authority; and this to me is more important than to hold office—to wisely and justly and kindly exercise its powers. I feel to say, may God bless her memory. She lives. She has gone to live. She is not dead. The first thing which struck my mind on entering this building was the beauty and appropriateness of these emblems, this white drapery, these beautiful flowers, these sprigs of green, which whisper not of death, but of life. White is God's mourning color. Winter is typical of death and when it binds the earth in icy fetters, God sends the snow, an emblem of purity and hope, to speak of coming Spring and life beyond. May God bless you my brethren and sisters. May He help us to emulate the noble example which our sister has left us. May we live worthy to meet with her and others of the just who have gone before, is my prayer through Jesus Christ, Amen.

APOSTLE HEBER J. GRANT.

As has been said by former speakers, there is nothing that I might say that could add to the

record that has been made by Sister Eliza.   I know
of no individual that has made a better record.   I
know of no individual whose every act has been
done with a desire for the advancement of God's kingdom.   I know of no individual in all my acquaintance that is more worthy of eternal blessings from
God, our Eternal Father, than our departed sister.
I do not feel to mourn to-day in the least.   I feel,
on the other hand, instead of mourning, to rejoice
that one that has labored so long, so energetically,
and so faithfully, has gone home to receive the
great reward that she is entitled to.   It is pleasing
to all of us, after we have labored for the accom-
plishment of anything on earth to receive the
reward, and it is a day of rejoicing to our sister,
that, after a long and useful life, she has received
the reward that she is entitled to.   It has been my
happy lot to be intimately acquainted with Sister
Eliza from my youth.   I have received many acts
of kindness at her hands, and much instruction.
I know of no sister in all Israel that has taken
the pains to bear testimony to me of the truth of
the gospel—with the exception of my own mother
—as often and as earnestly as our departed sister.
I have neither the language nor the ability to
express to you on this occasion the feelings that
fill my heart.   There is nothing so dear to the
human heart as the testimony of Jesus Christ,
and there is nothing that can cause that same
rejoicing to fill our hearts as when we know that
one that has this testimony borne unto her has
done nothing that would mar that testimony, but,

on the other hand, has day by day and year by
year grown and increased in that testimony. I
love good works and good examples. I am so
constituted that I rejoice in the labors and in the
good examples that are set by those holding res-
ponsible positions among the Elders of Israel or
among the sisters. I think more of good examples
than I do of precept; and I can say on this
occasion, and say it truthfully that there was no
example that was ever set by Sister Smith but
was worthy of emulation. I know that Sister Smith's friends are happy on this occasion.
They may mourn her loss, but they are happy in
the thought that she has gone to gain the reward
of a good record. It is a pleasure to labor for the
advancement of God's kingdom. Parents feel
anxious when their sons depart on missions, but
are pleased that they are worthy to go and proclaim the gospel to the nations of the earth.
Therefore, instead of feeling sorry upon this occasion, we feel to rejoice that Sister Eliza has filled
well her mission and will reap her reward. That
we may labor to accomplish the designs of our
Heavenly Father, is my prayer in the name of
Jesus, Amen.

PRESIDENT CANNON.

THE time has now arrived to bring these services to a close. I will, however, state the feeling
the deceased expressed shortly before her death.
She desired that no one should exhibit sorrow or
emotion at her departure; that if there should be

any drapery it should be white; that there should
be a few flowers if her friends felt to contribute them;
and that her coffin should be made of native
mountain pine. She maintained to the last all
the dignity of her womanly nature peculiar to
herself. She was also submissive to the Priesthood of God equally to the humblest daughter in
the land. And she was not only, as Brother Tay-
lor has said, a mother to this people, but was the
head of a large organization in the Church
known as the Relief Society of our Church. She
was sustained as such at our late Conference, and
to-day her absence is mourned by a people who
appreciate her worth. While we can congratulate
her upon her release, we feel to mourn her absence.

The choir then sang the beautiful song composed
by the deceased:

BURY ME QUIETLY WHEN I DIE.

When my spirit ascends to the world above,
To unite with the choirs in celestial love,
Let the finger of silence control the bell,
To restrain the chime of a funeral knell,
Let no mourning strain—not a sound be heard,
By which a pulse of the heart is stirred—
No note of sorrow to prompt a sigh;—
Bury me quietly when I die.

I am aiming to earn a celestial crown—
To merit a heavenly, pure renown;
And, whether in grave or in tomb I'm laid,
Beneath the tall oak or the cypress shade;
Whether at home with dear friends around;

Or in distant lands upon strangers' ground—
Under Wintry clouds or a Summer sky;
Bury me quietly when I die.

What avail the parade and the splendor here,
To a legal heir to a heavenly sphere?
To the heirs of salvation what is the worth,
In their perishing state, these frail things of earth?
What is death to the good but an entrance gate
That is placed on the verge of a rich estate
Where commissioned escorts are waiting by?
Bury me quietly when I die.

On the "iron rod" I have laid my hold;
If I keep the faith, and like Paul of old
Shall have "fought the good fight" and Christ the
    Lord
Has a crown in store with a full reward
Of the holy Priesthood in fullness rife,
With the gifts and the powers of an endless life,
And a glorious mansion for me on high;
Bury me quietly when I die.

When the orb of day sinks down in the west—
When its light reclines in the evening's crest—
When the lamp in the socket is low and dim—
When the cup of life is filled up to the brim—
When the golden Autumn's brief glass has run,
And gray Winter with whit'ning tread moves on—
When the arrow of death from its bow shall fly:
Bury me quietly when I die.

Like a beacon that rises o'er ocean's wave,
There's a light—there's a life beyond the grave;
The future is bright and it beckons me on
Where the noble and pure and the brave have gone;
Those who have battled for truth with their mind
    and might,

With their garments clean and their armor bright;
They are dwelling with God in a world on high:
Bury me quietly when I die.

Benediction by Patriarch John Smith.

The congregation passed in line around the casket and viewed the face of the dead.

The cortege which followed the remains to the private cemetery of the late President Brigham Young was formed under the direction of Bishop John R. Winder. Members of the High Council of the Salt Lake Stake of Zion acted as pall-bearers. Immediately following the casket were Apostle Lorenzo Snow and other relatives of the deceased, then the widows of the late President Young and other intimate associates of the deceased; following these were the members of the relief and other societies over which Sister Smith had presided, the general assemblage bringing up the rear.

At the grave Apostle Heber J. Grant offered up the dedicatory prayer, and President Angus M. Cannon, at the request of Apostle Lorenzo Snow, thanked the people for showing their respect for the deceased by turning out in such large numbers. The mortal remains of one of the noblest and purest women are now laid in their last resting place, to await the sounding of the trump of the resurrection.

The following beautiful verses were penned by Sister Snow a short time before her demise:

MY EPITAPH.

'Tis not the tribute of a sigh
  From sorrow's heaving bosom drawn;
Nor tears that flow from pity's eye
  To weep for me when I am gone:
No costly balm, no rich perfume—
  No vain sepulchral rite, I claim—
No mournful knell—no marble tomb—
No sculptur'd stone to tell my name.

A richer, holier tithe I crave
  Than time-proof monumental piers—
Than roses planted on my grave,
  Or willows dripped in dewy tears.
The garlands of hypocrisy
  May be equip'd with many a gem;
I prize the heart's sincerity
  Above a princely diadem.

In friendship's mem'ry let me live:
  I know no selfish wish beside—
I ask no more; yet, O forgive
  This impulse of instinctive pride.
The silent pulse of memory
  That beats to the unuttered tone
Of tenderness, is more to me
  Than the insignia of a stone:

For friendship holds a secret cord.
  That with the fibers of my heart
Entwines so deep, so close; 'tis hard
  For death's dissecting hand to part.
I feel the low responses roll
  Like far-off echoes of the night,
And whisper softly through my soul,
  I would not be forgotten quite.